When Love Heals

A Story of Healing from a simple touch of love

Written By

Inez S McRae

ISBN

Hardcover: 978-1-967668-28-1

Paperback: 978-1-967668-27-4

Forward

We learn about the healing power of Love from our relationship with God, who first loved us. We who love and know love will espouse love to another.

Characters

- Angela

- Damenian Hammonds...Brother Hammonds

- Chandler... a stationary store clerk

- Booker...Angela's Deceased Spouse

- Ava...Damenian sister

- Damenian's dad...Damenian Hammonds Sr.

- Christina...Angela's friend in church

- Myron...Ava Husband and Damenian's Brother - in - law

Every day we wake up to a new and unfamiliar day, unaware of what that day may hold for us. Angela remembers clearly when Damenian Hammonds (a member of her and her husband Booker's church) ended his marriage after a long sought after nasty divorce that turned out quite bitter after only 7 years of unhappy marital bliss. Brother Hammond's ex-wife soon remarried shortly after their divorce was finalized, and subsequently had a child with her new husband. Through everything, Damenian stayed loyal to his church and his duties as a church leader. Over the years, Brother Hammonds may have brought a woman to church with him once. But after that one time, he never came with anyone again. He always showed up alone, quietly, consistently, and without distraction.

Angela, who attended the same church as Brother Damenian Hammonds, had been married to Booker for over ten years. She felt secure and genuinely happy in their marriage. They enjoyed doing the things they loved, such as gardening, cooking on the grill, and entertaining, but most of all, they loved the comfort of their beautiful home. They lived modestly but spared no expense to create a home with stylish decor, featuring beautiful furnishings arranged in a magnificent layout. Angela exhibited great taste in home decor that was not limited to her personal fashion style in clothing, shoes & accessories. No one, not one person, would enter Angela and Booker's home without complimenting them on the well-placed decor, the color palette, style, arrangement, and staging of the home inside and outside.

Angela and Booker exemplified that they loved life and were living their best lives together, happily and uninterrupted. They often gave gatherings in the yard or on the deck and invited friends and family over. They would occasionally host a Friday Night Fish Fry, an Outdoor Turkey Fry, or light the Smoker and Grill Bar-B-Que with family and friends. Both Booker and Angela were loved for the numerous gatherings they held at their beautiful home.

Booker didn't like going to the doctor unless he had no other option or was already very sick. Even though Angela tried to explain that regular checkups were important for his health, he didn't listen. He ignored her advice and refused to take it seriously.

Angela and Booker lived their lives comfortably, giving many gatherings among friends, co-workers, and family in their lavish and beautiful home. One day at work, Booker felt out of sorts, unusually ill, and quite not his self. When he was unable to regulate his breathing, he was immediately taken to the hospital by ambulance. Booker stayed in the hospital for a few days undergoing many tests, which revealed a very serious condition that neither he nor Angela was prepared for. Booker was diagnosed with a rare prostate cancer that had reached stage 4 undetected.

As Booker began a long and tedious fight against this disease, Angela remained by his side, encouraging him, praying with him, and never once did she believe he could not win this battle. As the months passed, Booker became too sick to return to work. Even though he was receiving care and treatment from his doctors, the cancer kept getting worse, and his health continued to digress. No matter how difficult it was, Angela refused to place him in a care facility. She didn't want to leave him alone to let the disease run its course. Instead, she opted to have him treated at home in his wonderful home he loved so much.

Eventually, Angela had to have a full-time nurse to assist her with Booker's daily care. It was during this time that he lost his ability to walk or stand. Angela remained steadfast and committed to Booker as she curled up beside him each night in the hospital bed that was provided for him. Night after night, Booker fought a good fight against this debilitating disease. Angela remained at Booker's side, never leaving him alone, not for more than a second, until the day came when the disease took him. Booker died in his beautiful home after saying his final good night to his beautiful wife Angela for the last time before closing his eyes in eternal rest.

Booker's death left Angela all alone for the very first time in her life. Booker left Angela with a two-story $400,000.00 home along with three luxury cars parked in the driveway. Booker had planned well for the day of his demise; he had arranged for Angela to be financially taken care of and live in their home comfortably if she chose to do so. Booker often tried to teach Angela how to maintain small things around the house in the event of his absence. She learned how to use a paper clip if the thermostat stopped working and Booker showed her how to use the drill in reverse to remove screws. There were many things Angela never learned because she expected Booker to always be around. For example, she didn't know how to pump gas, since Booker always handled it. She would simply drive whichever of their three cars had the most gas and continue with her day. But now Booker is gone, and Angela is all alone for the first time.

After she buried Booker like a Royal King, Angela remained in the home, and she cried quite frequently. Angela spent her days inside her beautiful home, unmotivated, with very little energy, unhappy, bored, and crying most days as the days began to become intolerably long. Angela had a relationship with God, and she prayed as she looked to the Saviour for strength, protection, and guidance. Angela prayed and cried and prayed and cried some more.

A couple of months after Booker's death, Angela was still beside herself, living in unimaginable grief. She couldn't find her way, no matter how hard she tried to reach the warmth of happiness; she just couldn't find her way, so she remained trapped inside grief, loneliness, and sadness.

One day, many months after she buried Booker, Angela felt up to going to the supermarket when all she could find in the house was a single tea bag, no eggs, no bread, no food at all. So, Angela drove her SUV to the community supermarket, which she and Booker both frequented often over the years.

Angela pulled into the supermarket parking lot under the bright, shining sun. It felt refreshing, she was glad to be out of the house and in an open, breathable space. As she walked through the aisles, putting items into her cart, she suddenly began to feel a strange sensation that she couldn't quite explain. Suddenly, Angela knew she had better get out of this supermarket and do it fast; a crying spell was making its way directly to her, and she needed to hurry, so she immediately and quickly headed to the checkout line. Angela knew what was coming, a crying spell she would not be able to control or hold.

Without warning, Angela broke down into a fiercer crying spell than any she had previously experienced. As she stood in the supermarket checkout line, she had no choice but to let it out, and it came out loud. It was very emotional, gut-wrenching, and the tears flowed like a river, and Angela could find no human way to control them.

The employees and shoppers began to ask her what was wrong, 'Are you alright?' while another shouted, 'Get the store manager over here now,' which only made her cry even fiercer. Angela tried to convey to everyone she was alright; she just needed to get home. Angela then attempted to flee the grocery store, abandoning the items that the cashier had begun ringing up. Her exit was blocked by the store manager, who said to her, 'Ma'am, I cannot let you leave this store until the Police arrive.' They've been called; they will be here momentarily. If you could please come with me and have a seat until they arrive, I would appreciate it.

Angela and the store manager sat together until the Sheriff's Department Officers arrived. The two officers, upon arrival, immediately requested Angela's identification, showing no concern for her or her situation; they just wanted to verify her identity at that moment. After checking Angela's ID and running it through their system, the officers asked her what had happened. Angela explained that her husband, Booker, had recently passed away, and she still had moments when she broke down in tears. She told them she had run out of food and just wanted to make a quick trip to the supermarket and return home without any problems. She told the officers that when she made her way to the register, a crying spell engulfed her. She assured the officers that she would be fine once she got home.

At that time, one of the officers went into the supermarket and paid for the groceries she had left abandoned. The groceries totaled $57.00. Angela asked the officer how could she give him his money back, since she only had a debit card and no cash. The officer said to her I have a wife that I love very much and if something like this was to ever happen to her, I hope this gesture will be paid forward for her as well as to you. The Officers then followed Angela home in their patrol car, making sure she would arrive safely.

As Angela arrived home, the Sheriff's Department followed closely behind her, and the neighbors all came out onto their front porches to see what was happening. Ms. Loretta, Angela's elderly friend and neighbor, came running out from her home and across the street, screaming, "What did she do?" What did she do?" Angela turned to her neighbor as she climbed her front porch stairs and said, "Ms. Loretta, I didn't do anything except I started crying in the supermarket. They are ensuring I get home safely. I'll call you sometime tomorrow."

Ms. Loretta explained to the officers after she thanked them for seeing Angela home safely. She told the officers, Angela has been grieving for her husband for nearly 5 months, and she will talk with her to possibly get a little help with this. Ms. Loretta thanked the officers again for helping her neighbor before heading back across the street to her home.

Angela immediately felt so much better being back home, so she prayed and prayed, without ceasing, leaning upon the Word of God to help her through yet another night ahead. She knew the Lord Almighty would hear her cries and he would move her from the overwhelming grief. In the meantime, Angela handed it over to God and went to sleep.

After a week or two, Angela got up early on a Sunday morning and got dressed to attend Church for the first time since Booker died. Angela intended to attend church and hear from God. Little could she have known this day would be a defining day that would alter her's and another's life during their Individual losses that compounded both of their individual hearts with grief.

Angela attended Sunday services, sitting where she and Booker normally sat, which was on the left side of the church sanctuary. Her Pastor was so pleased to see her back in the service as he acknowledged her with a wave. As the church service commenced, Angela felt a huge crying spell welling up inside her. She knew immediately she must jump up and run to the church vestibule to release what felt to be her fiercest crying spell yet. She knew to breathe through it; she must release the tears that were welling up inside her, which she would have no human control over.

As Angela ran to the vestibule area, she immediately began to release tears of painful grief. With her head planted, in both of her hands on her lap, she cried in anguish. Church officials and ushers gathered around Angela, gently rubbing her back and fanning her to comfort her. But the more they tried to help, the harder she cried deep, painful sobs that clearly showed her heartbreak. Brother Hammonds stood nearby, watching quietly. He had never seen such a beautiful woman cry like that before. The women he had ever encountered were too shallow and vain to cry like that; their goal had been to make grown men cry in the dark instead.

Brother Hammonds immediately felt he needed to do something; he needed to help her. He got a white hand towel from the Pastor's chamber; he would then wet the hand towel with cold water. When he returned, he knelt down beside her and said to her, here, place this cold towel on the back of your neck; it will help you. Caught up in her emotional crying spell, Angela could not see him or the hand towel, so she lifted her hair and bent her neck to motion for Brother Hammonds to place the towel at the back of her neck for her.

When Brother Hammonds placed the hand towel against her neck; immediately, she felt a sense of something good, an unusual sensation that was comforting to her. She slowly began to ease her crying. Brother Hammonds began to gently massage the back of her neck with his hand placed on the towel as he whispered to her in a low voice, "Does that feel better"? She said to him, "Uh-huh, yes, it does". He said to her, 'I am going to wet the towel again, and I'll come right back.' She said, 'Okay.'

The ushers continued to fan Angela until Brother Hammonds returned with the hand towel, she once again lifted her hair to motion him to place and hold it to the back of her neck, again. As the crying completely ceased, she took the hand towel Brother Hammonds brought to her, and she began to wipe her face and the front of her neck. She thanked each of them for their consideration and concern in helping her. Angela asked one of the ushers if she could retrieve her belongings, her jacket and purse, which she had left behind when she went to the vestibule.

Angela assured everyone she was fine and would be even better once she got home. However, the church officials, including Brother Hammonds expressed serious concern about her ability to drive home alone. Brother Hammonds asked one of the church officials if he would follow him if he were to drive Angela home in her vehicle.

Brother Hammond's GPS provided him with the directions to the address she had given him, and he drove her car while the other church official followed in his car. As Damenian drove Angela home, she was curled up in the front passenger seat, facing the driver's side, covered up with her jacket. They didn't speak a word to each other throughout the ride to her house. Damenian consistently looked over at her many times, but said nothing to her.

Once they reached Angela's home, Damenian and the gentleman both walked her to the front door, where she fumbled with the key, her hands trembling, possibly due to the stress of crying. Damenian gently held Angela's hand with one hand and took her key with the other to unlock the door. As they stepped inside, both Damenian and the other man were amazed by how beautifully her home was decorated. They both said, "You have a very beautiful home." Angela smiled and thanked them for their kindness and for helping her. She assured them both that she would be fine and would be taking a well-deserved nap.

Damenian was so captured by Angela, he was mesmerized by her, he didn't want to leave her, he wanted to embrace her pass her heartbreak, he wanted to have her in a sincere, passionate way. When he finally came to his senses, he realized she was in grief over her husband's death, so he wished her a good night, and they left.

After a short week, Angela realized she needed help getting beyond the grief she was experiencing after nearly six months since Booker died. Angela immediately knew she needed to seek the help of the Elder Women of her church. Angela had come to terms; it was not healthy or normal for her to still be crying after such a long period of time. She unequivocally wanted help.

Without further thought, she reached out to the Elder Women of the church. Angela sent a text to Mother Carter asking if she and any other Elder Mothers could meet with her after Sunday service. In the message, Angela simply said that she needed their help and spiritual guidance. Mother Carter replied to Angela, 'We will meet with you on Sunday after service in the back of the sanctuary, at the last row on the right side of the church.'

On Sunday, after the service, Angela immediately headed to the back of the church, towards the last row of seats, as Mother Carter had instructed. Suddenly, five elderly women, dressed in wide-brimmed hats, beautiful suits, and matching shoes, surrounded her. As they began to sit down around her, they asked her, "What's wrong, Child?". Angela began to explain to them that since Booker died, she had placed great emphasis on "nearly six months ago", she couldn't stop crying, and she felt she was being held hostage by her grief. She told them she could barely leave the house because of her fear of being seen crying in public; she asked them, "Can you help me?"

The Women were all quite aware of her emotional breakdown last Sunday, which is why all 5 of them accepted her invitation to meet to help her. The elderly women all stepped away from Angela, and they talked to one another about how they would help her. They appeared to Angela to have already rehearsed for what they were gonna say, as if they had discussed this very topic among themselves before today's meeting.

The Elder Mothers were comprised of three widows like Angela and two who were still married to men of the church for more than 50 years. When the mothers returned to Angela, where she awaited them, they surrounded Angela and said to her, "We know what to do".

A rush of relief overcame her as she listened intentionally to these highly regarded regaled women. Angela trusted these women beyond any explanation, other than that God had placed and empowered their faith to know how to help her. Mother Carter said that, beginning this Tuesday afternoon, you will be joining us during our weekly meeting of the Elder Mothers of this church. I will send you a link to access our meeting, and you will take notes for us as our secretary. You will then forward those notes to me and a copy to the Pastor within a 24-hour timeframe. Mother Carter asked her, "Are there any questions or concerns?" Angela said no.

Hearing no concerns or questions, the Women stood in a perfect circle holding hands as they closed their meeting with Angela in prayer, asking God to lead the way in their endeavors and to bless the way he'll use, making all crooked roads straight. Each one of them said "Amen" and departed onto their separate ways.

Tuesday found Angela wide-eyed and very anxious; she looked forward to being in the presence of the highly regarded regaled women of the church. After nearly six months of grieving and crying, Angela began to feel a sense of renewal, thanks to the loving support she received. During her meetings with the Elder Mothers, she proudly and clearly wrote down the names of people who needed prayer, those who were sick, struggling with addiction, facing surgery, or dealing with abuse and other hardships. Requests received by each of the mothers via prayer text requests.

Damenian, still quite mesmerized by Angela, was pleased that she had returned to church and seemed to be better. Brother Hammonds became quite anxious to see Sunday's and his opportunity to see Angela from across the other side of the church, where he sat.

The following Sunday, when Angela happily attended church, the Pastor of the Church told the congregation that he was electing Angela to be the next Bible Study secretary, taking notes, commencing the following week. As the Pastor and the church congregation looked at her for a response to accept the appointment, the eyes of the Elder Mothers were on her nodding "Yes to accept. Angela stood and accepted his appointment.

Chapter 2:
So Begins the First Steps to Healing

We must understand that Angela and Booker both always believed their Pastor to be a divine man of God, so if he appointed any member of the church to a position, it was a well-thought-out plan to achieve some form of outcome. Angela immediately credited the Elder Mothers of the church because she believed they met with the Pastor and asked him to help her with this newly created position. Week after week, Angela took notes for both auxiliaries, and she typed and submitted them in a timely manner. Before she knew it, months had passed without a single crying incident. Angela finally felt, for the first time since Booker died, that she may have found freedom from what tried to bind her in grief, so she thanked God.

Angela began to feel the overwhelming positive effects of healing, a kind of healing in the name of the Lord, which felt refreshing. For the first time, Angela realized that Booker had planned for her to move forward in life without him, financially secure. When he was alive, Booker provided financial means to see that Angela would be alright in his departure from this life. He took measures and assured she'd be comfortable financially, far above what she could have imagined. Angela, after looking at the scope of what Booker did for her, she said, "Thank you, Booker." She wanted him to know she's okay now. It took a while to get to this point, but she's okay now.

After a few Sundays of Angela attending church, she was approached by Brother Damenian Hammonds after service. He asked her if she would go out to dinner with him. He appeared just a bit nervous, she looked at him like he was some sort of two-headed monster, unintentionally with the audacity to ask to go out so soon during her healing from grief and loss. Angela very kindly, politely, and softly declined his invitation and said, "Maybe another time."

For weeks, every Sunday, whenever Angela looked in Brother Hammonds' direction, he was already looking at her. At first, she thought he was just checking to see if she was okay or ready to step in if she started crying again. But as time went on, his constant staring began to make her feel uncomfortable. So, she stopped looking his way altogether, and after that, she had no idea if he was still watching her or not.

Angela had cleared a six-digit figure after all had been taken care of. Her $400,000.00 home mortgage was cleared to zero; she now owned her home mortgage free. She was grateful to Booker for his concise planning. Angela asked God for His mighty, powerful direction, guidance, and favor in her new endeavors to start a business that would benefit the well-being of the people she planned to serve. Angela began to set up the foundation of her Elegant and Sexy Plus Size Women's Garment Online Business, slowly, precisely, and concisely.

Angela created fashion for huge plus-size women, sizes 18 up to size 24. Angela's dream for the company she created was to take these women out of and away from their comfort area of hiding and covering up their sexuality. So, she dressed them in her exquisite taste in fashion. Her goal was to dress clients in elegant evening wear, including backless dresses for summer, strapless dresses for vacations, thigh-high front splits, one-shoulder apparel, spaghetti-strap garments, and a wide range of hand-selected, sexy tops specifically designed for larger women.

Angela created her newly formed company with an added personal touch that allowed her to teach her clients how to wear her garments fashionably. She was also available to them for questions and concerns 24/7. Angela's list to wear her garments looked like this:

1. You must make an investment in a good full-figure women's strapless bra...having a black and white one is preferable

2. You must also invest in an 18-hour full-figure girdle to make your curves smooth

3. You'll need to investment in a tape measure, knowing your bust, waist, and hip sizes will assure garments will fit accordingly.

Angela stocked her online company with the most fabulous, affordable, elegant, sexy, glamorous, plus-size apparel that she, and she alone, would hand-select.

Many days she spent searching for garments to add to her inventory took Angela hours upon hours because she only purchased what aroused her spectacular taste fashionably. Angela spent a lot of time searching from one supplier to another to find the right inventory. Eventually, her company officially launched and opened to the public. Shortly after the business began, Brother Hammonds asked her once again to go to dinner. He did not appear to be as nervous as the first time he asked her out, and she was no longer captive to grief; so much healing had taken place, and she thought he possibly recognized it.

Angela was in such a good place when Damenian asked her for the second time to go out with him, but unfortunately, she was entirely too busy to find time for herself in that way. She, in an apologetic soft tone of appreciation for asking, declined again, explaining to him she's just getting a new business started and there is just no time for herself at this moment in that way, but she hoped maybe another time. Damenian accepted her decline at face value while he tried to convince himself she wasn't just blowing him off.

Damenian began to confident in his church peers about his ever-growing feelings for Angela. He sought advice on what a prominent, self-made professional like himself needed to do to win the attention of the most phenomenal, beautiful woman who had ever captured his attention, for the first time in a very long time, if ever. Damenian slowly started to accept and realize that he truly wanted to date Angela, so he did the only thing he could do: he waited until she was ready.

Damenian worked as a senior manager for a very prominent company, owned an extremely nice home in an affluent community, he drove a white luxury Cadillac SUV, he dressed in fine nice suits and shoes, he was faithful to his church and God, but most of all he was *Single* not dating anyone at all. So, he asked himself what could make a beautiful woman like Angela blow him off? He decided to be patient, giving her a little more time, as he had been advised. Damenian watched her each Sunday from across the church sanctuary, the very same church they both loved and attended for years.

During this time, Angela's business was taking off, with orders for her exquisite clothing line that she had designed. One by one, her clients trusted Angela and allowed her to guide them into a new style of dressing, featuring colorful strapless and spaghetti-strap dresses and tops. She also sold fabulous two-piece swimwear, consisting of a one-piece swimsuit with a matching sarong wrap-around skirt in various designs and colors. Angela's business became an overnight success much faster than she could have imagined within her first year. Many of Angela's clients thanked her sincerely for changing their lives, for making them feel beautiful, and for her wonderful and fabulous fashion design. They became reliant on Angela to dress them for business, vacations, formal affairs, and casual occasions. One of her clients stated, "Angela has let the Jeannie out of the bottle, and it can never be put back in."

As her business began to flourish and take off both internationally and domestically, Angela started to love the positive feedback and the thank-you notes from her clients. She also loved making them feel elegant, sensual, and sexy.

Angela began to live for the business, and the business began to live through her, and that made her quite happy and very busy. She became the business, and the business became her; they were one, they needed one another to breathe, and to exist.

It was somewhere during this time that the business was becoming far more successful than Angela could have ever anticipated. When Damenian stopped her on her way to her car after church. He asked her how she and the new business were coming along. She replied, We're both great, up to our foreheads, trying to keep up with demand. He added, 'Congratulations on your success,' and she remarked, 'Thank you; it's a lot of work, but anything worth having usually is.'

As he looked upon her with total admiration, he said, 'I would like to take you to dinner to celebrate.' She looked at him, possibly admiring him too, and said, going to dinner with him would be nice, but she was entirely too busy to even catch up on some needed, well-deserved rest. So, he said hopefully they could make it another time when the timing would be better for her; she said yes and got into her SUV, driving away.

Damenian continued to accept her explanations for why she was unable to go out with him, and he also pondered whether she was just blowing him off. Everyone at church who knew the two of them and their history of grief encouraged Damenian not to give up on her, not yet. There was comfort in knowing she was not dating anyone; she was merely putting all she had of herself into her business. Damenian agreed with the advice given to him and found solace in knowing Angela was not dating anyone or blowing him off; he knew he truly needed to be the one for her. So, as he contemplated playing a role in Angela's life, he slowly began to realize he may be falling in love with her.

Requests for orders began flooding Angela's online business, both day and night. Angela soon discovered a stationery and shipping store where she could drop off her packages to be mailed to her clients, both domestically and internationally. She began making daily trips to this stationary business, when an employee there took notice of her and began having small, simple, kind conversations with her. He appeared to be smitten with her every time she came into the business.

Eventually, she found out the store clerk's name was Chandler, and he was quite attractive to Angela. Chandler was polite and greeted her whenever she entered his business premises. Angela soon became fond of his smitten greetings, and she began to like it. Soon, she could hardly wait until the next time to go to Chandler's place of business because she, too, had become smitten with him. Chandler woke up a part of her that now wanted to get dressed up, that wanted to look cute while maintaining her hair and makeup again. She began to calculatedly plan the outfit she'd wear when she was going there.

Chandler and Angela continued to show their affection for one another across the business counter that separated them. Angela suddenly entered the busiest season in her business's short existence. Starting during the Thanksgiving holidays up until Christmas through New Year's, Angela dressed her plus-size clients in the most elegant cocktail dresses for the formal company parties they would attend. Angela was mailing more than 70 outfits per week and making numerous trips to the stationery business she used to mail her clients packages. Angela also continued to take her secretary's notes each week for the two auxiliaries, as they remained her primary source of healing. The word of God was written in the notes she took, so she learned how to stand on the word of God. Angela had her hands full; she was beyond being very busy, and absolutely could not take on another thing, not even a single thing.

As Angela continued being busier than she could have ever imagined, wouldn't you know Damenian would be heading over towards her in the parking lot after church, looking as if he was going to stop her on the way to her car. Angela was aware of the number of times Brother Hammonds asked her to go out with him, and the number of times she had to decline. Angela quietly under her breathe said, "Jesus, take the wheel. You know I am too busy. Angela and Brother Hammonds both politely greeted one another. He said, "Sister Angela," and she replied, "Brother Hammonds." They small-talked about the weather before he stated to her, With so much going on with you nowadays, I am not gonna put you on the spot and ask you to have dinner with me, again.

She knew she needed to assure him, she would one day soon, so she literally promised him, as soon as her business exited the busy season she was in, she would let him know. Brother Hammonds, as always, said okay, but unknown to her, he decided to give up pursuing her; he was done. Brother Hammond's peers at church, whom he confided in about his feelings for Angela, pleaded with him, "Please don't give up on her, not now, Damenian, please not now". But Brother Hammonds' mind was made up, and he was no longer going to pursue Angela. He said to them all, "I'm done."

Angela continued to work tirelessly to near exhaustion, trying to keep up with high demands for her garments and her responsibilities to the 2 church auxiliaries she loved. She revered what was healing her.

Angela was nearing the end of her sales season for her elegant wear. She also noticed on Sunday that Damenian was no longer looking over at her from across the church, but instead he looked forward, purposefully, to ignore her. Angela's close friend at church was Christina. She had noticed how often Brother Hammonds stared at Angela during services. Christina would often gesture to Angela and whisper, "Why is Brother Hammonds always staring at you like that every Sunday?" Angela told her she assumed because he saw her cry after Booker's death, and he stopped her from crying; otherwise, Angela said she had no explanation for his staring at her in church.

On Sunday, Angela's church friend Christina headed over to her before she got to her car. Angela was so happy to see her friend after being so busy that she attempted to extend a big hug to her, but Christina grabbed Angela by the coat collar. She pulled Angela very close to her face and said, ***"Why won't you go out with Brother Hammonds?"***

Angela, being taken totally off her guard, answered, "For the same reason I haven't been able to return your calls, I've been too busy". Angela then went on to say to her friend, I promised him I would call him as soon as I finish up the last of my orders in about another week. Angela's friend Christina said to her after releasing Angela's coat collar and smoothing it out, ***"Just go out with him, Ange." Just do it!*** She told Christina, her girlfriend in Christ, that she would go out with Brother Hammonds.

It was 6 days before Christmas, December 19th, when Angela got the well-deserved break from her business. She had worked herself into total exhaustion and was completely happy with the business, far exceeding expectations in its first year. Angela wanted to celebrate; she wanted to go out somewhere to celebrate her accomplishments. She felt it would be the perfect opportunity to accept Brother Hammonds offer to take her out. Feeling an overwhelming need to celebrate anything since Booker died. She called the church secretary and asked her for Brother Hammonds number.

After Angela shipped the very last garment to her client, she sat down with a cup of herbal tea, and she called him (she called Brother Hammonds). Damenian was completely in awe, totally surprised when he answered the call and immediately recognized her phenomenally beautiful voice. They talked to one another for the first time; they talked for hours. They were both so comfortable, laughing, reminiscing about the church, about life, about being a Christian and Christianity, as well as gleaming through the phone with one another. The time had literally gotten away from them both. Although they had been members attending the same church for many years, they were never given an opportunity to have a conversation with one another like they were having now.

Angela managed to finally interject the reason for her call. She asked Brother Hammonds; she wondered if he was still possibly interested in going out with her. He immediately said to her, ***"please explain to me, what, no, why you are asking me such a thing"*** (she immediately recognized his funny sarcastic tone which she well deserved) she quietly laughed to herself and explained to him that the business had finally given her a much-needed break, and she wanted to celebrate her success, and he was the only one she had to call.

Damenian was extraordinarily ecstatic that she had called him; he said to her, "I am still very much interested in taking you out to dinner to one of my favorite restaurants." He told her he could pick her up in a few days because their dinner date required reservations. He also advised her to pack a bag, because it would be a full-day trip for them. He also suggested that she bring a dinner dress to change into for dinner. She quickly said to him that she had their pastor's number on speed dial, so no funny business. They both laughed and kept talking for a while before finally saying goodnight.

Damenian called Angela to pick her up for their dinner date the morning of Christmas Eve, December 24th, around 10:00 am. He drove his white luxury Cadillac SUV; Angela thought his vehicle was quite nice and comfortable for the 4-hour trip ahead of them. They talked to each other continuously, as Damenian drove them ever so closer to their destination.

Damenian was quite interested in knowing from Angela why she "Blew him Off" so many times over the last 18 months.

Angela assured him she doesn't "blow off people," and she surely never blew him off, never not instinctively. They continued to talk to one another even after they arrived at their destination around 2:00 pm in the afternoon.

They lunched, shopped, talked, and laughed before Brother Hammonds asked Angela once again why she chose to "blow him off" so many times, unable to think of a better way to phrase it to her. Angela assured him that it was simply a matter of timing and finding the right moment, which is what finally brought them to this point. Her answer seemed to ease Damenian's concerns, and he began to accept it. So, he let the matter go and stopped pressing her about it. They headed to the hotel suite, Brother Hammonds reserved for them to rest and change for dinner. Brother Hammonds had made dinner reservations for the two of them at a prestigious restaurant specializing in a variety of wonderful delicacies. Brother Hammonds was sure she would love the restaurant and find the 4-hour drive to be well worth it. Once they both unpacked their dinner attire, Brother Hammonds offered Angela all the time she needed to shower and get dressed for dinner, and he would wait in the lobby of their beautiful hotel for her to call when she was done, so he could come back and shower and dress too.

Once Angela was dressed and ready for their dinner date, she called Brother Hammonds to tell him he could come back to the room. Immediately upon entering the room, Brother Hammonds complimented how beautiful he felt she looked. Angela found herself increasingly impressed and interested in getting to know Brother Hammonds a little more. She thought what a gentleman he'd been to her, and how she liked it.

Once back in the suite, Damenian offered Angela to stay in the suite while he showered and dressed, or if she would be too uncomfortable for that, she was welcomed to wait for him in the lobby as he did while she showered and dressed. Angela chose to stay in the room while he got ready for their date. While Damenian showered, Angela checked in on her business, her messages, and emails. Brother Hammonds exited the bathroom with a towel wrapped around his waist. She tried very hard not to sneak a peek, but she could not resist looking at least once.

Angela was quite satisfied to see Brother Hammonds wore men's boxers; he was not a briefs man, and his upper body suggested he lifted weights quite frequently. Seeing no other reasons to sneak another peek while he got dressed, she was quite happy with her assessment of what she saw. Once Damenian was dressed and smelling nice, he reached out his hand for Angela to take, gently guiding her out of the room. They didn't have to go far to reach one of the most beautiful and amazing restaurants she had ever seen. A host led them to a quiet table set for two. The restaurant was only half full, primarily because it was Christmas Eve, which made their dinner experience even more wonderful for them both. They dined, they talked for a long period of time, and after they both finished their meal, they lingered there at the table with cocktails.

Damenian, then once again, questioned Angela about why it took her more than a year, nearly two years, to go out with him. She answered, his first request was too soon after Booker's death. She thanked him because when he put that cold towel on the back of her neck, she said it calmed her, his touch helped her to stop crying and she would be forever grateful; but no way in a radius of the next few months was she ready to go out with him or anyone else, she explained that's why she told him she would not be ready for that.

Angela went on to tell him, 'When you waited and asked me out again, I had just started the business. I had just begun to find my way, to build and plan the new stage of my life. I wasn't ready; I needed more time.' But I did say to you, hopefully, maybe another time. You waited a few more months and asked me again, but by then, the business was growing faster and becoming more successful than I ever expected. It just wasn't the right time for anything else. I told you I'd let you know when I was ready, and as you can see, we're here now because I called you, just like I promised. Angela then said to him, "So, for once and for all, I hope we can put away this idea of 'I wrote you off,' but instead, life happened to us, and we're here now."

Angela noticed the way Brother Hammonds looked at her, admiring her, and how he hung on every word, listening intently, not saying a word but taking in every word spoken to him in a starry-eyed kind of way. Damenian quietness put Angela on her guard because she knew not what this was leading up to. Damenian, finally breaking his silence, said to her that he'd looked forward to this very moment, to be alone with her, undistracted and uninterrupted, to be able to talk as they'd all day. He went on to say he had planned out in his head for more than 18 months how this moment would be relative to the two of them. He said once, maybe twice, I thought I needed to step away, just move on from you, but I couldn't and someone would always tell me, No, don't give up on her, give her just give her a little more time to find her way, and I'm so glad I listened.

Brother Hammonds said, Angela, this may seem a little too soon to you, and in that respect, I can completely understand, but it's been nearly 2 years for me. From the day I held that hand towel to the back of your neck, something happened to me, Angela. I have not been the same since that day. He said, Angela, what I am asking you, he hesitated for a moment and appeared a little nervous when suddenly he reached into his breast jacket pocket and pulled out a little black box.

Damenian stood up and then knelt on one knee. The black box opened, revealing a one-carat pear-shaped diamond ring. Angela grasped her mouth with both her hands in total shock. Brother Hammonds said, "Angela, will you please marry me?" I love you and want to continue to love you for the rest of my life. I would like to care for and protect you from ever crying like before. I want most of all to be your husband.

As Damenian knelt on one knee, the whole restaurant went completely silent. Everyone, both the staff and the guests, was watching her, waiting to hear her answer. She immediately thought this was too soon, after all, it was their first date. But to say no in public was not an option either, not while everyone was looking and waiting for her to respond to his proposal. She said yes, knowing that they would need to discuss this privately.

Damenian placed the ring on her finger, stood to his feet, extended each of his hands to her, and she placed each of her hands into his hands as he guided her to her feet. He kissed the back of each of her hands one at a time before he pulled her in close to him and kissed her with his soft, warm lips on her lips, and she liked it very much. A man hadn't kissed Angela in years, and she could hardly wait or contain herself for another kiss from Damenian.

They returned to the suite and decided to stay for the rest of the night. After all, it was Christmas Eve; they had just gotten engaged, and Angela desperately wanted and needed to kiss his soft lips again. During breakfast the next morning, Christmas Day, they finally had the privacy they needed to discuss their commitment to one another.

They both set the following agreements with one another. Brother Hammond wanted Angela to fully accept his loving her without setting limits or conditions telling him when or how he could show his love especially since he had loved her silently for almost two years. Lastly, he wanted her to give them a chance; he asked her not to return the ring, but to wear it while she got to know and trust him. Angela agreed to his well-spoken requests and decided to wear his ring, making no decisions to end their relationship or engagement without giving them a chance to know and trust one another.

Angela wanted to be very clear with Damenian that if she needed time, he would not try to rush her into anything she might not be ready for or prepared for. Damenian agreed to her request and assured her there would be no pressure; he would willingly allow her all the space and time she needed.

They concluded their breakfast, honoring their heartfelt commitment and agreements for each other. They both knew it was official; they were engaged.

The 4 hours it took them to drive home were far different from the 4 hours they rode down together. Angela's thought was that she was returning home wearing Damenian's engagement ring, and she had shared romantic moments with him that filled her heart with joy. Angela tried not to seem unimpressed with being engaged to Brother Hammonds, she felt he had to know this was a bit fast for her, but deep down in her heart, she wanted to honor her commitment to Damenian, she wanted to give them a chance, she wanted to get to know Damenian for herself, and she wanted to love him.

Once they returned home and back to their daily lives, Damenian and Angela began the process of getting to know each other. They talked to one another every day, and Brother Hammonds would occasionally visit Angela's house during his lunch break, which was normally a 2-hour break before he headed back to his office, and she returned to tending to her business. Sunday, after they returned home, Angela's commitment to one another became quite stressful. She's now more than just a church member to Damenian; she's now his fiancée. Angela was a little late getting to the church, but she made it in time before the service started. She entered the church sanctuary and spotted Damenian in his usual seat. As she walked down the aisle towards him, he turned, rose to his feet, and was overjoyed and quite ecstatic to see her. He stepped out into the aisle, extended his hand to her for her to place her hand in his, and gestured with his other hand for her to have a seat next to him. He gently put his arm around the back of her chair, knowing this was difficult for her as she sat next to him as his partner, in a relationship she hadn't had the chance to tell or show anyone yet. Nonetheless, he was proud of her, and he loved her.

During the service, their Pastor said he wanted to make an announcement. He asked Brother Hammond and Sister Angela to stand, please. He then told the congregation that the two of them got engaged to be married over the Christmas holiday. The congregation began to applaud them. He jokingly stated that Brother Hammond must know something about real love. Do you all see that big diamond ring on Sister Angela's finger? Angela raised her hand, proudly showing off her beautiful 1-carat diamond. The congregation clapped again, and many people came over to admire her engagement ring and congratulate them. From that day forward, Angela always sat next to Brother Hammond on his side of the church, and that made him very happy.

Damenian began to express his feelings with Angela living alone in her home, so far away from him in another county. Angela felt that ever since Damenian put his ring on her finger, he had begun to feel uneasy about her living more than 28 miles away from him and being alone. Angela and Damenian both understood unequivocally that living together must and will require being married. Angela had hoped for at least a 2-year engagement to Damenian. She totally understood Brother Hammond's concerns regarding her living situation, but there was nothing she could do about it.

Soon, Brother Hammonds and Angela's engagement approached its first 30 days, Angela began to change how she felt about marrying Damenian. She no longer needed to give him a chance to keep the ring on; instead, she wanted him, and she wanted to marry him as much, if not more, than he wanted to marry her. She began to love Damenian, really in love with him. About this time, Angela began thinking seriously about selling the house, about finally letting it go. She found a 3-bedroom villa apartment only 5 minutes away from Damenian's home. Angela put her home on the market, and it was under contract and sold in 20 days.

Angela moved into her spacious villa near Brother Hammond's home, and she agreed to marry him in 1 year, not the 2 years he felt was too long. They collaborated and agreed to get married on Christmas Eve, December 24th, one year to the date they got engaged.

Damenian and Angela grew close as a couple; they talked to each other every day since their engagement. After Angela sold her house, she moved to a new place, which was just 5 to 7 minutes away from Damenian's home. From then on, they always went to church together, riding in Damenian's car as a couple. Damenian had a key to Angela's apartment, and she had keys to his house and his SUV. What Angela really loved most about Damenian was his gentleman demeanor, especially the way he vowed he would not make love to her until they were married, no matter how badly he wanted her; he chose to wait for her.

Every day, they grew closer and fell deeper in love with each other. "Pack a bag, I'll be picking you up," never got old to Angela. She balanced both her growing business and her new relationship with Damenian, giving her love and energy to both. As time passed, Angela could sense that Damenian needed something to help him feel closer to their wedding, instead of feeling like it was still so far away. Angela discussed with Damenian about giving an elaborate Engagement Party, and immediately he fell head over heels for the idea.

Since their six-month engagement was just two short months away, they both had an awesome time planning the engagement party, which was to be hosted at Brother Hammonds' house. Halfway through the year, a mere six months before their wedding day, Angela was quite pleased to see that an engagement party was exactly what Damenian needed.

Angela spent most of her days at Damenian's house decorating his home with fabulous decor. Brother Hammonds loved Angela, her decor choices, and her ability to transform any space into something amazing. He excitedly agreed to anything she wanted; after all, it would soon enough be her home, which she would share with him once they were married.

They collaborated as a couple planning for their engagement party, they rented a champagne fountain, Angela had an exquisite menu catered consisting of: Whole Roasted Leg of Lamb and Roasted Duck served with various salads and streamed broccoli sides, she also had a tremendous fruit bar setup with various fruits displayed beautifully with every imageable fruit you could thing of; watermelon, cantaloupe, honey dew melons, numerous types of grapes in varying colors, strawberries, blue berries, raspberries just to name a few.

Damenian hired a person to smoke on the grill in his yard.. They smoked: BBQ ribs, Chicken, Steak, and steamed Lobster tails, all on a couple of huge smokers. Damenian and Angela collaborated on the design of the banner, which read, "Congratulations Damenian and Angela, engaged on Dec 24." They verbally invited guests; they wanted to print no invitations. They invited family members, members of the church, including the 5 Elder Women, friends, and many of Damenian Co-workers. They requested a church announcement to invite anyone who wished to join in celebrating their engagement.

Their engagement party was set for the 2nd Saturday in June, and it was an absolute success. Those who attended the engagement party considered it the best party of the year. Damenian and Angela spared no expense to share with everyone who knew them, they found each other and soon will become husband and wife.

That evening, when the engagement party ended and everyone had departed, Damenian and Angela were completely exhausted. Unintentionally, they fell asleep, cuddled in each other's arms, fully clothed, for the entire night.

Late in the morning, when they woke and had breakfast, Angela said to Damenian, "We have only a short six months left to plan for our beautiful wedding, our wedding night, and our entire life together. Damenian said We'll just continue to save up our love for one another until our wedding night; we will let our love and our passion for each other explode on our wedding night." They kissed, hugged, cuddled, and told one another, "I love you," and immediately began discussing plans for their wedding.

Over the next 6 months until their wedding day, both Angela and Damenian were hands-on with planning for their special day. Brother Hammonds and Angela both agreed they wanted to have an unconventional, non-traditional wedding for their 2nd marriages; they both even elected a non-traditional day to take their vows before God on Christmas Eve. They both wanted to say their vows in a church, standing at the altar in God's sanctuary. Without any hesitation, they agreed to get married at Damenian's parents' church, the same church where he was raised. Angela thought it was the perfect place. It was cozy and just the right size, not too big or too small, and it fit perfectly with their wedding plans.

During a weekend visit to his parents' house, Damenian and Angela secured the church for their wedding day. The church stewardess toured with Damenian, Angela, and his dad, Damenian Hammonds Sr., taking notes on what she needed from the church. Angela remarked to the stewardess that nothing more was needed, with the exception of her flower choices and arrangement. Damenian and his dad both stood behind the two women in the background as they watched Angela intently as she described her vision for her wedding flower arrangements to the stewardess, who took notes.

Angela expressed she wanted royal blue and white to be her leading flower colors, and since it will be Christmas Eve, she wanted to adorn their wedding with poinsettias of various colors. She said she wanted it to be full and lush, even if artificial flowers had to be used. Damenian interjected with his authoritative voice, saying, "Whatever she wants, give me the bill; I'm taking care of anything she wants."

Both Angela and the stewardess who wrote that down turned around to Damenian. Angela thought to herself, "No, he didn't just say that in front of his dad in such an authoritative way," and immediately she thought, Damenian's marriage to her will become a lifetime honored by the memories of how much they loved each other. They chose to have a 4-member wedding party consisting of the two men and 2 women who diligently told Damenian not to give up on Angela, which alternately brought them to marriage.

Angela chose Royal Blue for her wedding dress color. It was beautiful and sure to knock Brother Hammonds off his feet. Angela chose to wear a sheer top long sleeve thigh high front split, she dressed Damenian in a white tuxedo jacket with black pants and a royal blue boutonniere for his lapel, the men in her wedding party she adorned in all black tuxedos with the same royal blue boutonnière, she then dressed the 2 female members of her wedding party in royal blue spaghetti strap knee length dresses with matching short cropped length jackets and white pearl necklaces and pearl earring.

Damenian's mother and his sister, Ava, were hands-on with helping Angela and Damenian; they found both a local baker and a caterer. Angela and Brother Hammonds family particularly his mother grew quite close to Angela in such a short period of time. Damenian dad, Ava Damenian's sister, Ava's husband, Myron, and finally Damenian's mother all loved and embraced Angela with the love of gratitude for having her in the family. Damenian's mother could undoubtedly see that Angela loved her son and how Damenian loved her too. Angela brought out a new and better version of Damenian, his family had never seen. Damenian and Angela developed a habit of telling each other "I love you" every day, sometimes several times a day, and they would also kiss one another every day. The way Damenian and Angela loved each other was quite pleasing to his family.

During the wedding planning stages, Damenian's mother suggested that Angela's wedding party spend the night at her home before the wedding day, along with Damenian and her. Damenian parents had a huge, cozy, and warm home. That thought took off, and other members of the family said they too would spend the night before the wedding at Damenian's parents' home. Damenian began to bring air mattresses to his parents' home to accommodate the folks who would be staying overnight to attend his and Angela's wedding on Christmas Eve.

As Angela and Damenian continued to plan their wedding with the help of his mother and sister, Angela decided that on the morning of her wedding, she wanted to have a huge breakfast catered for all those who stayed overnight, those who were coming to town, and those who were staying in a hotel.

Angela and Damenian had scheduled their wedding for 11:00 am, so she wanted the caterers to begin serving breakfast around 6:30 am, so the sweet smell of bacon and sausages would wake up anyone.

Damenian and Angela both spared no expense for their wedding day breakfast, and it would be rememberable for a long time to come. Omelets were made to order, pancakes were placed on the griddle to order, up to 6 versions of sausages, grits-n-shrimp, fruits, and many versions of apple and orange juice were served. It was a flawless hit. Everyone enjoyed the food with family and friends, some still in their pajamas, having breakfast before getting dressed to witness Damenian and Angela take their wedding vows. Once breakfast concluded, Angela had the caterers stay and clean up and prepare for the meal to be served to her guests at Damenian's parents' house after the wedding ceremony.

Damenian and Angela once again spared no expense for their wedding day meal; they served everyone who came to his parents' home. They had a huge, garnished Roasted Turkey, Roasted Lamb, Beef Ribeye Roast, and Chuck Roast, along with multiple and various side dishes.

After their vows were taken before God in the sanctuary, the photographer took plenty of pictures of them, their family, friends, and the wedding party. Damenian had arranged for the church van to drive a couple of their church members to the wedding. The church van was used to take the wedding party back to their cars at the church, no later than 4 o'clock, so they arrived home to be with their families for Christmas.

Damenian parents' friends continued to come to the house with wedding gifts, Christmas gifts, to mingle, to partake in the exquisite catered meal while they sipped champagne openly in celebration. Damenian and Angela stood close together in the center of the open living room, wrapped in each other's arms. They danced to one love song after another, never stopping. They moved so slowly and so closely that it almost looked like they weren't moving at all, just swaying gently to the music.

As guests continued to come to Damenian's parents house they stopped, pointed and admire the newlywed couple in the middle of the floor closely, slowly dancing to love songs still in their wedding attire, Damenian's mother said, " don't y'all pay them no mind, they are in love with each other, you'll get used to it". A couple of moments later, a few couples joined Damenian and Angela in the Living Room Den area, moving every bit as slowly and closely hugged up in love, like them to love song after love song..

Damenian whispered in Angela's ear, "I love you, Ange." "I love how beautiful you look," he then whispered to her, "Thank you, Baby, for the best day of my life". Angela kissed Damenian on his neck just below his ear lobe, and she whispered in his ear, "I love you, Dame, I always have, and I always will. Thank you, baby, for the best day of my life". She kissed him passionately on his warm, soft lips, and they continued to dance for a few more seconds. Damenian then took a step back, admiring her phenomenal beauty, when he stretched his hand out to her, and she placed her hand in his, and they exited together hand in hand.

As Damenian and Angela went to get their coats, he gently helped button Angela's coat to keep her warm. Then he grabbed his own coat, leaned in to kiss his mother on the cheek, and said, "Save a plate of food for me and Ange. It's been a long day, and we want some time alone, so we're heading over to the suite (a 4-star wedding suite, of course)." He promised his mother he and Angela would be back tomorrow on time for the family Christmas Dinner festivities at his parents' house, but he could not promise they would make it to the family breakfast in the morning.

Upon Angela's returning from the church after the wedding, she had the Cater's pack her and Damenian an exquisite meal into thermal warming bags to keep warm, a bottle of champagne along with glass champagne flutes, and a single Rose, and a single candle holder to signify their first night of marriage together. She then had the Cater's to load it all in Damenian's car for them to take to the bridle suite.

When Damenian and Angela arrived at their beautiful 4-star bridle suite, they put the exquisite food in the dining area of their suite. They both began to strip immediately until they were both nakedly embracing one another. They made love for the first time as husband and wife over and over all night while they repeatedly said to each other, "I love you" over and over until they just fell into exhaustion.

Christmas Day Damenian and Angela missed the family breakfast that morning as they anticipated they would. They were there early for the family Christmas festivities. Angela heated up breakfast foods Damenian mother had put away for the two of them. For the first time during the holidays Angela was with Damenian and his family as his wife, and for the first time in so many years Damenian was with his family and he had a wife for Christmas.

Angela and Damenian with her business remained very happy and in love, they remained happily married for many years ahead of them, always taking the time to tell one another every day "I love you". Not a day would go by without Damenian and Angela both thanking God above for hearing their individual cries, for bringing them together, healing them and blessing their marriage.

The End